ANIMAL Sanctuary

Dear Reader

I visited a penguin sanctuary before I wrote this book. I really enjoyed it. I hope that you do, too.

The penguins that live at the sanctuary are happy and healthy, and very well looked after. When you first see them, it's hard to imagine that each and every one of them has been injured or has a disability.

THE PENGUINS THAT LIVE HERE ARE HAPPY AND HEALTHY …

These physical conditions prevent them from surviving in the wild.

The penguin sanctuary is a great place because it lets the penguins live a good life. It also lets us learn a little more about these beautiful birds!

John Parsons

My sincere thanks to the following people for their time, information, images and enthusiasm for this book:

The rangers and staff at the International Antarctic Centre, Christchurch, New Zealand.

NELSON
CENGAGE Learning™
For learning solutions, visit **cengage.com.au**

Contents

ANIMAL Sanctuary

page 4

1 Are We at the South Pole?

Follow the trail of blue penguin prints. Will they lead to the South Pole or to the International Antarctic Centre in Christchurch, New Zealand?

Pages 6–7

TEXT TYPE
Explanation

2 Feeding Time

Find out what happens when it's time to feed the penguins – it's quite a process!

page 6

page 10

3 Working with Penguins

The people who work with penguins tell us many things about their feathered friends. And, find out why ranger, Jo, looks closely at penguin vomit!

4 A Penguin Romance

Penguins usually stay together for a long time. But penguins always choose a mate with the best song and singing sounds!

page 14

5 People Who Help Animals

Many people dedicate their time to helping and caring for animals with special needs.

page 18

SCIENCE FEATURE

Injured Penguins

What to do if you find an injured penguin.

page 21

6 Packed with Penguin Facts

Dive in for some amazing penguin facts.

page 22

Index and Glossary page 24

1 Are We at the South Pole?

An **Antarctic** Experience

Imagine flying high above snowy mountains. The pilot throttles back the engines and you begin to descend.

Minutes later, you're stepping off the plane. You gather your bags and head outside.

Follow Blue Footprints

You follow a trail of blue footprints on a brick path.

follow these blue footprints

As you walk, you see a giant aircraft used by the United States Antarctic Program. Ahead of you is the building where people prepare to travel to polar stations.

the US Antarctic Program hangar in Christchurch, New Zealand

The USA, Italy, New Zealand and other countries all have polar stations here.

An All-Terrain Snow Vehicle

From your right comes the roar of a powerful engine. It is an all-terrain snow vehicle. It rumbles forward on its heavy rubber tracks.

an all-terrain snow vehicle

some of the sights that will greet you

The International Antarctic Centre

You have come here to learn about the Antarctic. You will:

- dress in clothing designed for sub-zero conditions
- experience the chilly howl of a polar winter blizzard
- hear the voices of polar explorers
- get up close to the penguins, as they sing, swim and feed together.

You might be wondering if we're at the South Pole … but we're not. We're in New Zealand, 5000 kilometres away.

This is the International Antarctic Centre, in Christchurch, on the east coast of the South Island of New Zealand. Here, visitors can learn about what it's like to be in Antarctica. They can also see little blue penguins.

2 Feeding Time

waiting for lunch

sprats

looking for fish

A **Natural** Diet

Ensuring every penguin receives proper nutrition is an important part of the work of the penguin rangers. This helps to keep the penguins happy and healthy. How do they manage to ensure this is done?

Planning the Food

First, the rangers plan the penguins' food to ensure they get all the nutrition they need. They know that penguins in the wild like to eat small fish and other sea creatures. Small fish, such as sprats, are the main part of the penguins' diet at the sanctuary. This means the penguins' diet is as close as possible to what they would eat in the wild.

catching a fish

Still So Fast!

No one would ever guess that almost every one of the penguins at the sanctuary is either injured or has a disability. Some are blind, while some have only one flipper or one leg.

Preparing the Food

In the food preparation area, the rangers measure and weigh sprats and herring. They need to ensure there is enough food for every penguin. Then, at the same time every day, they get ready to feed the penguins.

The 26 little blue penguins also know exactly what time it is – feeding time!

Jo, a ranger

diving for fish

Feeding the Penguins

Jo, one of the rangers, then carries a bucket of sprats and herring over to the pool. Because the penguins catch and eat food underwater, they shuffle to the edge of their huge pool, and dive in.

As you can see, the penguins at the sanctuary are given a healthy, balanced diet to ensure that they live for a long time. The penguins seem to love feeding time, as they dive and turn like torpedoes beneath the water.

Penguin Care

One Fish at a Time

It's important that every penguin is fed properly. Jo doesn't just throw fish into the pool. Instead, she drops the fish into the pool one at a time, in different places.

Jo explains to the visitors why she feeds the penguins one at a time, so everyone understands what is going on.

Record the Fish Eaten

As each penguin catches a fish in its beak, Jo calls out its name. A volunteer helper writes down how many fish each penguin eats. By keeping careful records, the rangers can make sure every bird gets enough food every day. By the time the bucket of fish is empty, Jo will know that all 26 birds have had something to eat.

After Feeding

After feeding time, Jo looks at the list with the helper to check that every bird has been fed. The penguins climb out of the pool. Then they sun themselves on the rocks while they digest their food.

one at a time

see what is eaten

time to digest the food

Extra Care for Penguins

By comparing daily records, the rangers can be sure all the penguins will stay healthy and well fed. They are also able to tell if a bird has lost its appetite or is eating more than usual. This might be a sign of illness or injury, which they can then check out.

PENGUIN SIZE

Little blue penguins are the smallest species of penguin. When fully grown, they stand about 40 centimetres tall and weigh about one kilogram.

Questions and Answers

Before Jo leaves the pool area, she answers questions from visitors who come to the penguin sanctuary. Because feeding time is popular with visitors, Jo can answer many questions like:

"***What does it take to work with penguins?***" asks one visitor.

"***You need to not mind getting dirty,***" says Jo.

question time

Finally, Jo checks her bucket for leftovers, and makes a joke. "***Does anybody want a raw sprat? You have to eat them whole, just like a penguin!***"

The visitors laugh, and head towards the cafeteria. The real human food is much better!

FOOD IN THE WILD

In the wild, penguins eat small fish (like krill), squid, shrimps and other small sea creatures.

3 Working with Penguins

Penguin **Identification**

When a new penguin arrives at the sanctuary, it can be difficult to tell whether it is a male or a female. Males tend to be a little bit larger and taller. But, as Jo explains, often the only sure way to tell is to see who lays an egg!

Penguin Tags

Jo explains how she is able to tell which penguin is which.

"Each penguin has a small, coloured tag to identify it," she says. "Male penguins wear their tags on their left flipper. Female penguins wear their tags on their right flipper."

She also explains that pairs of male and female penguins share the same colour tags. Staff then know that they are "boyfriend and girlfriend".

Gilly (left) and Jo (right) with a little blue penguin

Study Animals Closely!

Jo trained as a zoologist, a scientist who studies animals. At university, Jo did some research about penguin vomit!

"I was surrounded by vats of frozen penguin vomit!" she says. "It was a good way to find out about what penguins ate in the wild."

Jo feeding the penguins

> "I WAS SURROUNDED BY VATS OF FROZEN PENGUIN VOMIT!"
> JO

A Safer Environment

Some of the penguins at the International Antarctic Centre came to the sanctuary because they were ill or disabled. Some of the birds had been attacked by cats, dogs, stoats (weasels) or ferrets. Many of the birds have been injured by boats. Because they are steely blue, they are very hard to spot in the water, so boats accidentally hit them.

Orlando's Injuries

Jo points out one penguin. "That's Orlando," she tells us. "He was hit by a boat. It broke his collar bone and knee bone. His bones have healed, but every day we try to make his muscles stronger with special exercise."

Little blue penguins recover at the sanctuary.

Penguin Predators and Hazards

In the wild, sharks, seals and killer whales can kill little blue penguins. On land, they are at risk from certain birds, such as large gulls and sea eagles. Humans also cause many problems. Oil spills, plastic, car traffic and fishing nets can all injure or kill the penguins.

a killer whale (orca)

Survival

None of the penguins here would have survived in the wild. Jo and the other rangers help them live a safe and healthy life at the sanctuary.

Jo educates visitors that come to the centre about the dangers to little blue penguins from humans and introduced animals.

4 A Penguin Romance

How Do Penguins **Choose** a **Mate?**

Gilly

Another person who works at the International Antarctic Centre is Gilly. While I am talking to Gilly, one of the penguins starts to sing. A penguin's song sounds like a cross between a deep, throaty pigeon and a warbling hen or rooster.

"That's Alex," says Gilly. "He is singing to try and find a girlfriend."

An Injured Penguin

Alex was attacked by a dog or cat, and has a paralysed flipper on his left side. This means he has trouble swimming straight. But there's nothing wrong with his singing.

Listening to which penguin has the best song is one of the ways that penguins choose their mates.

Alex

I SWAM UP TO LISTEN OUT FOR THE BEST SONG!

A Singing Competition

"Alex and another penguin called CC used to be a pair," explains Gilly. "But one year, CC chose another penguin to be her mate, because he sang better."

What was the name of the penguin who was a better singer? Elvis!

Alex spent hours outside CC's nest. He tried to win her back with his singing, without success. Alex wants to find a new mate as it's breeding season.

Breeding Season

The breeding season for little blue penguins starts in August. Usually, the male penguin picks out a burrow to nest in. The penguins use sticks, leaves and long strands of flax to build a nest. Females lay two eggs between September and November. Both birds take turns sitting on the eggs to keep them warm.

Some penguins can stay in pairs for up to ten years, but not CC. About a third of them change partners during their lifetime.

Arts and Music

Elvis Presley (1935–77)

Elvis Presley was a very famous rock-and-roll singer. He is remembered as the King of Rock and Roll in music and movies.

Elvis Presley

MAORI NAME

The Maori name for the little blue penguin is *korora*.

Alex Keeps Trying

Alex shuffles along the row of burrows that lead to the nesting spaces. His song sounds deep and throaty. None of the female penguins are interested in being Alex's girlfriend.

He gives up for the day.

At least he is not lonely. Penguins prefer to live in large groups. With 25 other birds, Alex has plenty of company. One day, Alex will find a new partner at the sanctuary.

Alex shuffles along a row of burrows.

Arts and Music

Happy Feet – the Movie

Happy Feet is an animated musical. It tells the story of a misfit penguin. He has a talent for dancing instead of singing. In the film, he learns that every penguin must sing a "heartsong" to attract a mate. If the female likes the male and his song, the two penguins stay together and raise chicks.

Some of the movie characters are based on Adélie penguins like those in the picture.

Alex's Bright Future

In the wild, it would be extremely difficult for a disabled penguin to survive. Alex will spend the rest of his life at the sanctuary. There's plenty of fish and there are no predators. He is kept healthy and happy.

It's as if the sanctuary is a dream come true for Alex!

PENGUIN LIFE SPAN

The average life span of a little blue penguin is about seven years. However, some have been known to live for up to 20 years.

MAKING ALL MY DREAMS COME TRUE ...

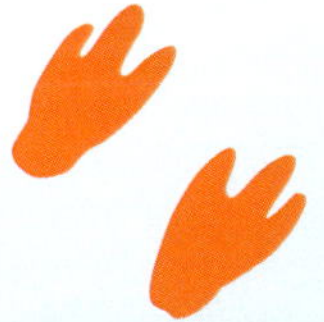

5 People Who Help Animals

Animals with Special Needs

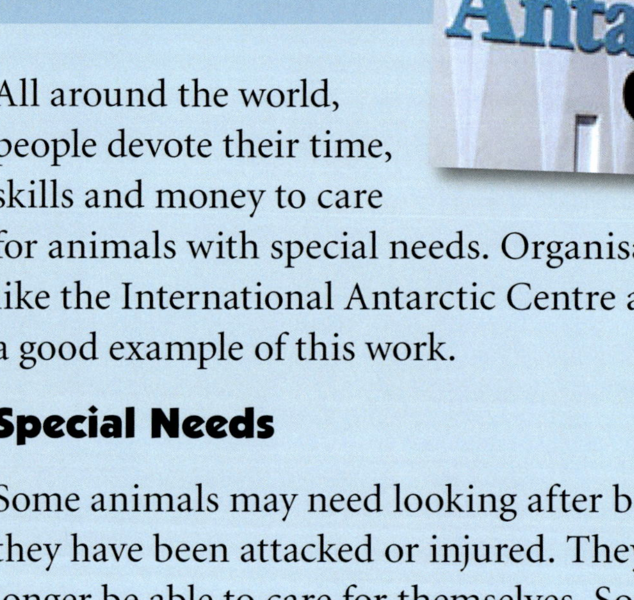

All around the world, people devote their time, skills and money to care for animals with special needs. Organisations like the International Antarctic Centre are a good example of this work.

Special Needs

Some animals may need looking after because they have been attacked or injured. They may no longer be able to care for themselves. Some may have grown old or become ill. Some animals who once had owners are abandoned. They may not have the skills needed to survive alone.

Sometimes domestic animals need care, too. Others are abandoned. Their owners may not be able to look after them because of problems with their health or behaviour.

FEATHERS

The feathers of little blue penguins are indigo blue and slate grey. The feathers are oily, which makes them waterproof.

Gilly and Jo tend to a penguin's needs.

Sanctuary Care

If some animals do not get special care, they will die. Others learn to adapt to their injury or disability, and survive. Some animals that need extra care will be fortunate enough to find themselves in an animal sanctuary.

At the International Antarctic Centre, people like Jo and Gilly work to provide a place where penguins can live safely and comfortably.

Penguin Education

The staff and volunteers at the sanctuary also enjoy educating visitors. When people learn about how their actions can affect animals and their environment, they may need to change their behaviour.

Time to Go

As we leave the sanctuary, we head back through the International Antarctic Centre. Here we pass by the simulated snow blizzard.

Outside the frozen room, a red digital clock counts down the seconds until the next blizzard. During the blizzard, the temperature will drop to minus 20 degrees Celsius.

Time for a Blizzard?

There's just time to scramble into a pair of snow boots, waterproof leggings and a thick, insulated polar jacket. Feeling like a well-padded penguin, I walk towards the door.

And then …

But wait,
that's another story!

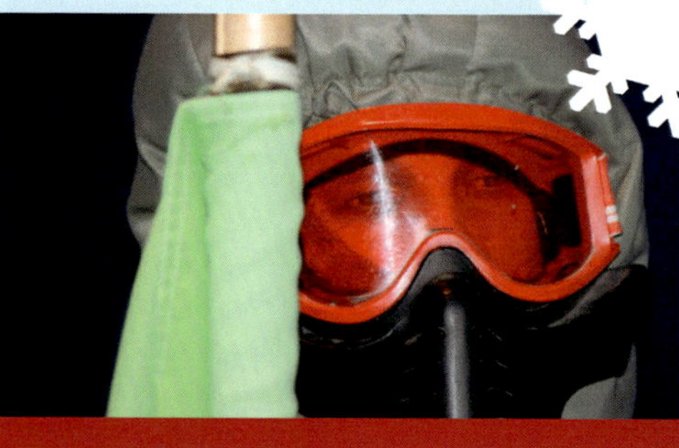

BLIZZARD

A blizzard is a severe winter storm, with low temperatures, strong winds and heavy blowing snow.

Earth and Space Sciences

Antarctic Storm

Very few people can go to Antarctica and experience its awesome and magical beauty.

The storm at the International Antarctic Centre blows every 30 minutes in the "Snow and Ice Experience". It provides an authentic Antarctic blizzard with winds up to 40 kilometres per hour.

Warm jackets and over-shoes keep people warm as the temperature drops to minus 20 degrees Celsius.

blowing up a storm

SCIENCE FEATURE

Injured Penguins

If you find an injured penguin, stop and think. Keep yourself safe first. The penguin will be frightened and distressed. It may use its beak to protect itself if you startle it.

Make a Home

If you believe a wild animal like a penguin needs help, the general rule is to keep it warm and quiet. A box with an old towel in the bottom is a good place to put the penguin. Make sure there are air holes and a lid.

Be Gentle

Wear gloves, or use a towel, to gently pick up the penguin. Provide some fresh water for the penguin to drink. If the animal is tangled in a fishing line or plastic, do not try to untangle it. You may injure it even more.

Injured animals rarely need food, so don't attempt to feed it.

Seek Help

You should contact either a vet, an emergency clinic, a sanctuary or a wildlife centre at once.

an injured penguin at the sanctuary

Packed with Penguin Facts

A Penguin **Quiz**

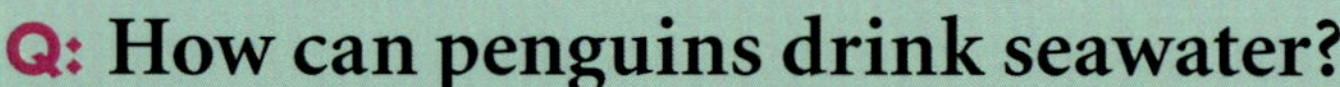

Q: What do penguins drink?

A: Penguins can drink seawater when they are thirsty. For birds that spend up to 75 per cent of their lives in the sea, this is very useful.

going for a swim

Q: How can penguins drink seawater?

A: Penguins have special glands that filter out the salt in the seawater. The salt is then removed through tiny grooves on the bird's beak!

Q: How do penguins stay warm?

A: Penguins, like all birds, are warm-blooded. They need to keep their bodies above 37 degrees Celsius. In the icy Antarctic, this can be a challenge! They have a layer of fat under their skin called "blubber". They also have a layer of fluffy, soft "down" feathers covering their skin. The feathers on the outside of a penguin overlap and are covered with an oily substance. Like a good raincoat, they form a shield to keep the warmth in.

Q: Why do penguins huddle together?

A: Often, when it gets really cold, penguins will huddle close together for warmth. As many as 5000 penguins can huddle together in a group to keep warm.

penguins huddle together

Q: Why are penguins white on their underside?

A: In the wild, penguins have many predators. In the sea, killer whales, leopard seals and sharks all eat penguins. The penguin has white feathers on its underside so a predator swimming below the penguin will have trouble seeing it against the white ice above.

the black and white penguin suit

Q: Why are penguins dark on their upperside?

A: Predators, such as sea eagles, also hunt penguins. When a penguin is swimming in the dark water, its dark upper feathers blend in to the colour of the sea. That makes it hard for birds to spot them from above!

Q: What's the largest penguin?

A: The largest is the emperor penguin, which can be over a metre tall and weigh up to 40 kilograms!

emperor penguins

Q: How fast can a penguin swim?

A: A penguin can swim at speeds of up to 40 kilometres an hour.

Q: How far can a penguin swim?

A: Most penguins will swim between 15 and 50 kilometres a day, searching for food. A penguin holds the record for swimming over 100 kilometres in a day!

Q: Can penguins fly?

A: No. But they can jump. When a penguin wants to leap out of the water, it can jump almost two metres to reach the ice.

Index

Antarctic 4, 5, 20, 22
Antarctica 5, 20
International Antarctic Centre 5, 12, 14, 18, 19, 20
penguin
- diet 6, 7
- food 6, 7, 8, 9, 21, 23
- nutrition 6

polar
- explorers 5
- jacket 20
- stations 4
- winter 5

predators 13, 17, 23
South Pole 4, 5

Glossary

Antarctic	The name referring to the features and environment that can be found in the continent of Antarctica
burrows	Small tunnels made by animals such as penguins
introduced	Animals or plants that do not naturally occur in a place, but have been brought there by people
nutrition	The correct amount and types of food, vitamins and minerals needed to keep something healthy
predators	Animals that survive by hunting and eating other animals
sanctuary	A place where animals unable to survive in the wild can lead safe and healthy lives
volunteer	A person who helps out by working or offering their skills without getting paid